ADVENTURE HUNTERS

Tales Of Imagination

Edited By Wendy Laws

First published in Great Britain in 2022 by:

 Young**Writers**®
— Est. 1991 —

Young Writers
Remus House
Coltsfoot Drive
Peterborough
PE2 9BF
Telephone: 01733 890066
Website: www.youngwriters.co.uk

All Rights Reserved
Book Design by Ashley Janson
© Copyright Contributors 2022
Softback ISBN 978-1-80015-930-3

Printed and bound in the UK by BookPrintingUK
Website: www.bookprintinguk.com
YB0502N

FOREWORD

Are you searching for adventure? Then come right this way – fun and daring deeds await! It's very simple, all you have to do is turn the page and you'll be transported into a wealth of amazing adventure stories.

Is it magic? Is it a trick? No! It's all down to the skill and imagination of primary school pupils from around the country. For our latest competition Adventure Hunters, we gave them the task of writing a story on any topic, and to do it in just 100 words! I think you'll agree they've achieved that brilliantly – this book is jam-packed with exciting and thrilling tales.

These young authors have brought their ideas to life using only their words. This is the power of creativity and it gives us life too! Here at Young Writers we want to pass our love of the written word onto the next generation and what better way to do that than to celebrate their writing by publishing it in a book!

It sets their work free from homework books and notepads and puts it where it deserves to be – out in the world and preserved forever! Each awesome author in this book should be super proud of themselves, and now they've got proof of their ideas and their creativity in black and white, to look back on in years to come!

We hope you enjoy this book as much as we have! Now it's time to let imagination take control, so read on...

CONTENTS

Danesfield CE School, Williton

Effie Ellwood (10)	54
Ruby D'Alcorn (10)	55
Grace Mcloughlin (10)	56
Evie James-Allen (9)	57
Thomas Ellicott (9)	58

Ennerdale CE Primary School, Ennerdale Bridge

Heidi Edmondson	59
George Lister (9)	60
Jessie Torrance (8)	61
Olivia Hyland	62
Annabelle Fye (10)	63
Elwood Park (10)	64
Jorge Edgar (11)	65
Beatrice Parkinson (8)	66
Stanley Baxter (9)	67
George Stitt (8)	68
Jude Naven (8)	69
Nieve Fye	70

Fairway Primary School, Mill Hill

Fabian Gontaru	71
Maryam Gitey	72

Glenboig Primary School, Glenboig

Olly Pender (9)	73
Hollie Wood (9)	74
Tianna Hornal (9)	75
Abigail Doig (9)	76
Cameron Shaw (10)	77
Jane Mitchell (10)	78
Murdo Neil (9)	79
John Brown (10)	80
Emma Kennedy (10)	81
Kieran Cummings (9)	82
Ala Mleczak (10)	83
Jemma Pickering (9)	84
Connor Maloney (10)	85

Rhona Struzik (10)	86
Jodie Taylor (10)	87

Handcross Park School, Handcross

Pranav Khurana (8)	88
Maggie Lunn (10)	89
Zac Jones (8)	90
Aneira Cook (8)	91
Tennessee Milkins	92
Shreya Chitrapu (8)	93
Lucy Flatt	94
Harriet Higginson (8)	95
Evie Gilbey (9)	96
Aroha Jagnale (8)	97
Leo Howells (8)	98
Florence Clusker-Artemis (9)	99
Cecilia Rivera (9)	100
Angus Weightman (8)	101
Henry Sheikh (8)	102
Chloe Dawson (8)	103
Connie Lunn (9)	104
Chloe Smith (8)	105
Lucy Clark (8)	106
Evelina Jansen	107
Harry Haswell (9)	108
Matilda Hewitt (8)	109

Kennoway Primary School, Kennoway

George Page (8)	110
Cole Vanbeck (7)	111
Lyla Stevens (8)	112
Danni McFarlane (8)	113
Nathan Scobie (8)	114
Kieran Cramb (8)	115
Anna McMenigall (8)	116
Jake Smith (8)	117
Corey Lambert (8)	118
Lily McDougall (8)	119
Reilly Clader (8)	120
Gordon MacDonald (8)	121

THE STORIES

The Phoenix Of Embers

The three friends (with their hot chocolate, of course) read through the book of myths.

Their beady eyes had attention on the article about the legendary Phoenix of Embers. It was so interesting that they were almost forced to read it aloud.

"The Phoenix of Embers has awoken. Enemies of the Embers, beware."

They had opened a portal to a reversed world, the oceans had been reversed with lava and tsunamis were surrounding them. Though... they were protected. Warm flaming wings and a towering kind of bird screeched a melody that made the waves cease. We'd found it... the phoenix.

Alice Saikowski (9)

Abbey Catholic Primary School, Erdington

The Abandoned Volcano

The three friends were about to enter the abandoned volcano when... *stomp!* They landed hard. The volcano crackled and snapped. The deathly light shone into the black hole of clouds. They walked on and heard the death-defying screeches of the unknown. The biggest most terrifying shadow covered the glazing beams of light. They turned around to see the red crimson colour all over their friend, they knew they were walking into danger. Slowly they strolled into the deadly darkness. All of a sudden a creature crept up behind them. The three explorers were never seen... but their bones still lay.

Josie Lynch (10)
Abbey Catholic Primary School, Erdington

Heaven Or Hell?

"I'm sorry." Lilly could not believe that Jeff killed her sister. Lilly ran off crying not looking where she was going. *Crash!* Lilly thought to herself, *what just happened?*
Jeff came with a knife. "You should have stayed," Jeff whispered.
Lily closed her eyes. Surprised she woke up but she was not on the island. She saw an angel and it said, "Heaven or hell?" She chose heaven. It seems Jeff came soon after, he went to hell. Lily visits him sometimes but she will never forgive him and will stay with her sister in heaven forever.

Eva Lily Swords (9)
Abbey Catholic Primary School, Erdington

The Mystery Of The Abandoned Hospital

On one stormy night, two private investigators set off to scrutinise the mystery of the abandoned hospital. Will they become successful, or will they not? They both arrive at the hospital. They enter. They stay still. Creaks were heard by both of them. Instantaneously, they were both captured! What will happen next? Thoughts raced through their minds.

A spy and an explorer, who are now ex-rivals, team up to discover what has happened to those two. They both explored the hospital. This will choose the fate of the whole world. They suddenly found them and freed them. All is safe.

Jaeden Gauss Modelo (10)
Abbey Catholic Primary School, Erdington

The Secret Of The Dragon

As they entered the gloomy depths of the dragon's cave they heard the roar of the mighty dragon.

"Who's in my cave?" said a booming voice.

They walked closer to see a giant monster. They started to run with the monster behind them. They ran there, here and everywhere. Suddenly, a sharp pointy tail grabbed them from their back and started to fly.

"Don't be scared of me, I'm friendly," said the dragon. "I'm not the one who killed your friend."

They then saw a human with blood dripping from everywhere, who killed her...?

Paloma Jinesh (10)

Abbey Catholic Primary School, Erdington

Oliver The Pig

One night, aliens teamed up with talking fruit to take over the universe, but then Oliver the pig came! "Not for long!" said Oliver the pig.
"You can't stop us," said the strongest alien!
Oliver the pig ate the talking fruit and beat up the aliens! "Hooray for Oliver the pig! The universe is now saved!"
"We will come back, and when we do we will win!" said the aliens.
Oliver the pig is the best superhero in the whole world! And that is it... for now! But Oliver the pig will defeat the aliens' comeback!

Daniel Kiernan (9)
Abbey Catholic Primary School, Erdington

A Death In The Dark

A death-defying creak filled the house. The door opened as if someone had done it for me. "Hello," I asked trying to see whether anyone was home. Blood was splattered all over the wall. I could tell because it had that dark red crimson colour. But what was that hiding in the shadows? "Hello," the thing said in a creaky voice, "who are you and what are you doing in my house." It was now shouting. "If you don't get out of my house in five seconds I'll kill you! 3, 2, 1," said the voice. Suddenly I was dead!

Isabel Bragington (10)

Abbey Catholic Primary School, Erdington

The Prickly Plant

Ever since we moved to Dublin, strange noises came from the house around the corner. So one day I decided to investigate.

I stepped in through the shattered window and cold, dusty air filled my asthmatic lungs. I heard screeches from upstairs. I ventured into a narrow, filthy room that smelt of chemicals and an omen of death. A storm was now growing large out of the cracked window, a prickly vine came shooting through and seized me by the neck making multiple miniature slits in my throat. It lifted me up and dangled me outside. It dropped me.

Luca Joyce (9)
Abbey Catholic Primary School, Erdington

The Virus And The Book

I didn't notice a hole while walking down the forest, so I stumbled into it.

It felt like I fell through the whole world and when I stopped a bright, glistening light shone onto an object looking similar to the book of spells we are looking for... "It is it!" I got up and took the book, and with my last wish I teleported back to the root of the virus, I chanted the sentence of destruction and the virus was gone.

My mum ran back to me and cried hard, I didn't notice my friends were dead.

Antonina Przybyla (10)
Abbey Catholic Primary School, Erdington

The Dangerous Forest

In the creepy, forbidden forest lay a mighty colossal dragon who was very dangerous. The fire-breathing dragon was as high as the cotton candy clouds which turned dark after the dragon breathed fire all over the little section of the forest. This scary dragon lived in a dark, gloomy cave, when you enter the forest all you can hear is the loud roars of the dragon. This forest is like no ordinary forest, it's dark and scary and you would not want to enter it unless you want to be defeated by the dragon...

Niamh Toland (10)
Abbey Catholic Primary School, Erdington

City On The Sea

On a warm beach day, two friends, Mavis and John, were on a beach. They were sitting and saw a shiny pearl. When they went to look they got pulled in. They saw a mermaid, she was head of Seashell City. She was not nice. She said in a deep voice, "Come now." When they approached her two mermaid guards came and took them to a deadly sea monster no one had ever killed. They were meant to kill it. They took a pearl and *bang*, it was dead. The mermaids gave them a gift of a magic sea pearl.

Victoria Maleki (9)
Abbey Catholic Primary School, Erdington

The Death Of Laura Rose

1895

In New York, Laura Rose was a pilot in the 1890s, the best of humanity. On the way to work, she got a call from her boss at the airport. She had to fly to a mysterious island with no name. As she started to ready up her plane nobody noticed that a tiny, little screw had fallen out. Later she began the journey. "Plane 5 is going overboard, repeat Plane 5 is going overboard," cried Pilot Laura. A few moments later, the plane was found underwater with nobody to be seen...

Bella-Rose Willetts (9)

Abbey Catholic Primary School, Erdington

The Legendary Cure

There were two rusty, old levers, one would drop the cure, but the doors would close. The other lever would open the door. I chose the first lever. (The second lever wouldn't drop the cure.) Rocks began to fall quickly. Three levers appeared, I needed to pull them in a certain order. There were the colours, red, orange and yellow. I pulled them in the order of the rainbow. The exit opened and I ran. I gave the cure to my family but they faked being sick so I could have an adventure.

Aidan Lynch (9)
Abbey Catholic Primary School, Erdington

A New Place

Walking on the grim cement, a horrendous odour engulfed the drenched plants as they slowly developed crunchy, dry petals. While that occurred outside, inside, melodious hums invaded the silent, pitch-black setting. As dense as metal, a stale, infected crescent of bread thundered away through the terrifying, innocent bird's timid, lumpy chest. This gruesome lifestyle was opened as the 'explorer' chucked the bush on the ground stowing away from his boarding school knowing this might now be a place he would be accepted. Suddenly on the horizon, a corrupted storm brewed heading towards him... He had to run...

Tehzeeb Chowdhury (11)
Beeches Junior School, Great Barr

Reality

It was dark. She couldn't see her hand. Well, she could move it at least. Was she awake? Silly question, she was awake... wasn't she...? She couldn't move. Was she paralysed? No, she remembered the night before, the early morning, the horror from the fact how Annabelle was gone forever... Suddenly, she could feel the wind blowing in her blistered face, she was actually there. Faster than a cheetah, a cylinder sailed through the sky and landed right next to her, it brushed up against her, she couldn't move! Another! Right into her chest and *poof!* White, light, reality.

Xiyan Baig (10)
Beeches Junior School, Great Barr

Among Us Who Is The Imposter?

Seven people in the room, one of them is an imposter. They will be killed one by one until there's only one left! Crewmates complete tasks (to fill their taskbar) while the imposter vents from room to room on a killing spree.

One mistake and the imposter vents in front of the crewmate and it is game over. A crewmate rushes to the emergency meeting button to discuss what he saw.

Crewmates vote or skip while the imposter tries to convince the crewmates that he isn't the imposter. Eventually, the imposter gets voted out and ends up revealing their identity.

Amelia Welcome (11)

Beeches Junior School, Great Barr

I Harnessed A Force

It was a dark, damp night. I tried to be furtive (it was past my curfew). I stumbled into directions to somewhere. I followed the directions and I observed as closely as I could. It was a brick wall; I looked even closer and accidentally jolted forward and something changed. Imminently, a mammoth, medieval manor appeared. I entered, the amount of dust was grotesque. I heard a loud cacophony... I stood there paralysed to my fear.

There was a mysterious room. I saw a glowing bubble of energy. I touched it reluctantly... Now I have a power like no other.

Sawan Banger (10)
Beeches Junior School, Great Barr

The Monstrous Creature

There once was a wise, kind King, who had a robust, brave son, who really wanted to kill a creature. He sent loads of strong armies but their efforts were helpless. One day, the people in the palace were petrified that the green, slimy monster was going to break into the palace. The King told his son to go to the cave (where the creature lives) and kill it so the anxious people would calm down. He walked for a long time until he finally reached the dark, eerie cave. In no time the monster died. They lived happily after.

Dhaval Champaneria & Dylan Trow (10)
Beeches Junior School, Great Barr

I Found A Power

As I woke up in my comfortable, soft bed I went downstairs to have breakfast (toast and eggs). I ran as fast as lightning to school and it seemed like a normal day (but was I wrong). As I ran I caught a glimpse of a genie's lamp on the ground. Immediately I grabbed it, I opened it hoping for a genie to come out but this mystical light came out and blessed me with special powers.

The next day I found out my power was more than one. They were fire and ice powers. I shouted, "I have superpowers!"

Shuaib Razzaque (11)

Beeches Junior School, Great Barr

Jude's Superpower Story

As I woke up in my comfortable bed, I ran downstairs to grab my bag. I shouted bye to Mum and ran to school since I missed the bus. I got into class and I was late so quickly put my stuff away and sat down.

A couple of hours later, school finally finished. I walked back home and found a golden lamp on the floor. I hoped a genie would come out. I rubbed it three times and a genie popped out and granted me superpowers (ice, fire and water). I jumped up and down happily and ran home.

Jude Witsey (10)
Beeches Junior School, Great Barr

Breaking Out

Two days in, I'm still in prison. I keep on thinking someone will save me, but they won't. I still think a miracle will happen but it won't. I have five days until my execution for a crime which I didn't even commit. No one believes me. This prison is really secure but, there has to be a way out!
The next day, as I was walking to my cell, I saw a vent. This wasn't just any vent, it was a vent which led to outside. I tried escaping, but the vent was stuck.

Arib Majid (10)
Beeches Junior School, Great Barr

The Dead Devourer

The Destiny's Bounty was flying quickly over Scattered Canyon. On the Bounty was Lloyd, Kai, Jay, Nya, Zane, Cole and Wu. In hot pursuit was Pythor on Rattlercopter with the snake, Scales. They were heading to Oroborus. At Oroborus there was the serpentine doing a slither pit battle. When the Bounty got to Oroborus there was a humongous battle! Pythor got the chance to unleash the Devourer, he was heading to Ninjago City. When the ninja arrived there was a humongous battle! At the end of the fierce battle, Lloyd cut the Devourer's head off. Everyone was happy.

Henry M (7)
Camelsdale Primary School, Camelsdale

The Cave Of Death

The rain was blowing around the dinosaurs. Woolly and Sloth ran into a cave to get shelter but in front of them was poisonous gas. There was someone there... It was Woolly's friend, Wolal. When they saw her they breathed! They started laughing from the gas. They were scared. Wolal saw a zip line and tried to pull but she needed more animals. There was a sound, it was coming closer. Who was it? "It's Buddy! This is good," said Wolal, "let's pull." They got them out.
Sloth said, "Let's go to bed," and they went to bed.

Andrei Salisbury (7)
Camelsdale Primary School, Camelsdale

Barry The Investigator

One day, Barry was investigating a crumbled mine. He heard rain. Barry could feel his heart pumping. He did not know what was going to happen. He was shaking with fear. Barry could feel the uneven walls of the rough mine. It was getting darker. But he was only going to light a flickering match if something really dangerous happened.
Suddenly he fell into a pit of slimy snakes! He lit a hot match and all the steamy, misty smoke trailed through the mine and came out. His friend Milo saw the smoke and called the police. He was safe.

Freddie Phillips (7)
Camelsdale Primary School, Camelsdale

Sandstorms

Sandstorms were blowing all around and all over the hot Sahara desert. Pyramids were boiling with hotness crumbling all around. I marched through until I came across an old abandoned village. I went inside one of the tombs. I saw thousands of shelves full of gold, silver and fools gold. Suddenly I heard a big crash I looked outside and saw the way I had come in had collapsed. I tried not to panic when I saw robots marching towards me. I ran back in and saw another way out. I marched back with a souvenir forever.

Freddie W (8)
Camelsdale Primary School, Camelsdale

Hunter Boy

Once a very long time ago in the windy mountains, there was a strong boy called Dagger. He was half thunder god, half-man. He had a gold staff and an ugly witch was coming after it. He was trying to get all the souls she had stolen. *Boom!* She got to the silver village, got the golden staff and got away. She then tried to find more golden staffs. Dagger followed her to the massive castle. He found the glowing souls and got away. He went back to the silver village and gave the glowing souls to the gods.

Micah H (8)
Camelsdale Primary School, Camelsdale

The Little Bird

A bird lived in a forest, he loved to eat food. His favourite food was delicious worms. There was a storm. The lightning flashed on the ground. He flew home as fast as he could. Unfortunately, his home was knocked over. It was dark so he needed somewhere to sleep. He found a shelter and he fell asleep.

In the morning the storm was still raging. In the corner of his eye, he saw a key. He picked up the key with his pointy beak and shook the key. Miraculously, the storm disappeared, so he was happy again.

Cherry-Mae Ward
Camelsdale Primary School, Camelsdale

Lava Invasion

On the cave walls it was lashing down with rain and Pepper and Freddie realised that the floor was hot. It was lava! They rushed outside. They used boulders to block it but it did not work. Suddenly, they realised that there was a path underground to the sea. They dug down until they joined up with it. The lava crept in and they watched for hours and hours but Freddie said it was taking too long. Luckily, he spotted a lake and they dug a path to the lake. Water covered the lava and it disappeared!

Rafe Walder (7)

Camelsdale Primary School, Camelsdale

A Haunted Monster Cave

Soldier Sam was walking to a haunted monster cave, then he was right in front of the cave. He looked scared but he went in. He had a sword to protect him from the beast. He was called Crosser. He was very hard to kill. He was very purple. Sam went deeper into the cave and he saw purple bats. They were the Crosser's guards. Sam had a torch. He shone the torch at Crosser. Crosser fell back. Soldier Sam pushed his sword in and he was dead. Sam was very proud of himself for going into the cave.

Sidney B (7)
Camelsdale Primary School, Camelsdale

The Amazing Power Hunt

One day I found an amazingly fluffy werewolf. I was scared but then it said it was really friendly. The werewolf took me to his friends. They were monsters but someone had taken their powers so we had to find the person who stole them. We searched and searched until we found a house which had a witch inside. She had stolen their powerful powers. When it was night we planned to break in and destroy the pot with the powers. We broke in and had to break the pot. *Bang!* The pot was broken.

Isla Wareham (7)
Camelsdale Primary School, Camelsdale

The Laser Sea

On a very small remote island, there was a seven-year-old boy called Rex. He had somehow drifted to the island and he needed to get off it. First, he was hungry, there was a little berry bush and a big palm tree. He picked some berries. Then he found out that there were lasers in the sea. He had to dodge the lasers. He dodged and swam for a very long time. At one point he stopped on another island but then started swimming again. After a very long time, he found land. Then Rex went to sleep.

Arin Zachariah (7)
Camelsdale Primary School, Camelsdale

The Glitch

I got up to see a glitch. I found that the world was turning into cubes! I also saw a horse and a note at the end of my bed! The note said, 'Take Honey home'.

I left and saw a key in a tree and a giant gate connected to a wall.

Clonk! "Ow!" The key hit my head. "Ow!" The padlock fell on my head too. The door opened. I got on the horse, fell off then got back on. We went to the big red words that said... 'Game over!' Oak, my dog licked me.

Francesca H (7)
Camelsdale Primary School, Camelsdale

The Boy, The Malinoi And The Wolf

A year ago in a mini world, a boy called Tom lost his timber wolf, Zach. He tried everything he possibly could to find him. Then he had a spectacular idea. It was to go to Zach's favourite place by the river. He used his Belgian Malinois Rio to sniff out Zach. Tom gave Zach, who was covered in squelchy mud, some delicious treats. Tom gave Rio some treats for finding Zach. They all snuggled up by the cosy and crackling fire.
The next day they all woke up to a new beginning.

Aidan Clement-Riley (7)
Camelsdale Primary School, Camelsdale

The Scared And Lost Mermaid

There once was a sparkly, happy mermaid called Coral. Coral lived in the calm coral reef. It was very pretty and colourful.

One day she went out of her house, she swam and swam so far she did not know which way to go home. Coral was so worried that she could not think. But then she thought of somebody who could help. It was her best friend, Seaweed, she could tell her where to go. Seaweed said, "Yes I can help." So Seaweed took her home to see her family again.

Erin B (7)
Camelsdale Primary School, Camelsdale

The Curse

I've heard about a curse that died a long time ago. It lived in the desert and the sand still has little specks of dust. I went to every desert, but I couldn't find a single speck of dust.
One day I saw a tiny speck of dust glow in the sand so I picked it up! "Yay." I was so happy. I went behind a bush to look at it and put it in a glass jar. I got some wood and built myself a warm shelter for the night. "I did it. I completed the quest!"

Tommy Rouse (7)
Camelsdale Primary School, Camelsdale

The Magic Key

On a crisp morning, I woke up to the sound of huge crashing waves. I was in the deep dark ocean. Then I found a sparkling key, it was a magic sparkling key but then I lost it. I was very upset. The next frosty morning I found myself in the deep ocean again. Finally, just when the sun went down I found the key, I was so happy. I swam very fast back to the crisp yellow and brown shore and went straight to sleep.
The next morning I realised it was all a big dream.

Eleanor E (8)
Camelsdale Primary School, Camelsdale

The Volcanic Race

One day in a deep jungle I was in a cave lifting stones. I was only seven and the stones were heavy. But then I was disturbed by loud roaring, I rushed to see it was a tiger! The tiger was white and it could not swim so I helped the tiger out. He said, "Thank you." I jumped. He told me that he wanted to go to the top of the volcano. So we walked, ran, skipped and jogged all the way to the top. But then the volcano erupted and we ran all the way to my cave.

Ollie G (8)
Camelsdale Primary School, Camelsdale

Cave-In

Once in the deep dark jungle, Oli was in a cave sitting by his fire with his wolf. One day Oli and his wolf found a mine. In there he found a piece of gold then a cave-in happened! They were trapped for weeks.

After a few weeks, Oli had a plan. The plan was to climb out. He gave up but he saw light until a big rock fell down! He was all right but he could not get up. Oli pulled up on an oak tree root and climbed out. He went home and went to bed.

Oli M (7)
Camelsdale Primary School, Camelsdale

Milo And The Big Bubble

Once I woke up and found gum under my bed. I started chewing on my gum. When Delia (my sister) came in and scared me I swallowed my gum! I was walking to school with my friend Freddie. I told him I swallowed my gum but he didn't believe me. So I took a breath in and a humongous bubble came out. I started to fly. I fell asleep. As soon as I woke up I was on a giant mountain! Suddenly I saw a rainbow yeti! I jumped on its back but it ran away.

Milo Cox (8)
Camelsdale Primary School, Camelsdale

The Volcano Cave

I was walking in a cave on the side of a volcano! It was dangerous but nothing happened. I kept on going until I saw the end of the cave. But it was the start of the cave. Why? I went back but I just came back to the start. I knew what was going on, I was going in circles. I went back but I went the opposite way and I saw the end of the cave! I ran, ran, ran and ran I got to the end of the cave. I ran back home.

George Archer (7)
Camelsdale Primary School, Camelsdale

The Swamp Demon Game

Once four kids magically appeared in a video game. A strange voice said, "You're in a video game, to get out slay the demon!" They prepared by making weapons, then set off on their journey. They ventured through volcanoes, forests and rivers. They came across a smelly swamp! Suddenly the horrifying demon appeared out of the dark depths.

"We aren't afraid," they shouted. They charged at once. Two of them managed to get their weapons into his heart, killing him in a matter of minutes. Then the strange voice said, "You have won, now you can live your normal lives."

Florence Meek (8)

Cawood CE Primary School, Cawood

Volcanic Eiffel

Yassen Polesky was eating his lunch, when he saw Vladimir Sharkovsky sprinting towards the bus stop, cautiously looking behind him. Yassen leapt up from his table to follow Vladimir. The two walked up Volcanic Eiffel, Yassen ducking behind every boulder, determined not to be seen. Yassen arrived at the top. With a sudden jolt, he realised the tyrant Sharkovsky wanted *the Gem of Eternal Life*! He sprinted inside the volcano, desperate to reach the gem first. He did, but, as he leapt for the gem, Vladimir shoved him. He and the gem tumbled into the lava. He died a hero!

Oliver Thomas Davenport (11)
Cawood CE Primary School, Cawood

The Mermaid, Bubbles And The Billionaires: The Underwater Adventure!

The Hindmarches zoomed through the sky on their jetpacks. They could see the choppy waves beneath them! Suddenly, their jetpacks started to splutter, and they plummeted into the sea. Fortunately, their buddy, Bubbles the whale came along and they rode on his back. After hours of swimming, they stumbled upon an old boat holding a mermaid and lots of gold! Together, they sailed back on the tattered boat with Bubbles beside them. The mermaid became famous for being the first to ever be seen by humans, and the Hindmarches became rich yet gave all the money to save the whales.

Holly Hindmarch (10)

Cawood CE Primary School, Cawood

Amazon Adventure

Once upon a time, four children had a plane crash and landed in the Amazon rainforest. They felt disorientated! Awaking in the rainforest the next day they instantly became intrepid explorers. This included: catching fish, climbing pineapple trees, furthermore seeking fresh water. Unfortunately, Felicity fell in the water! She panicked and began to sink like a brick! Luckily Amber dived like a mermaid into the unknown water and saved Felicity. Spluttering and choking they rested on the riverbank. Finally, they heard a noise in the distance! It was help!

Amber Smales (9)
Cawood CE Primary School, Cawood

Hector Saves The Planet

Hector our hero heard the news of a massive asteroid heading towards Earth. *I must do what I can to save the planet,* he thought. He went to his father who worked at NASA to see how he could help. "My team could build a rocket to stop the asteroid from hitting Earth."
The day came to launch the rocket. "5... 4...3... 2...1... blast-off." Up went Hector in the rocket into space. He managed to collide with the asteroid pushing it off track. It was a near miss, the Earth survived and Hector was a hero. "Hooray."

George Freeman (9)
Cawood CE Primary School, Cawood

The Train Murderer

It was a long train journey and every now and then the lights flickered. It was the fifth time that the light had flickered that I noticed that every time the lights flickered someone died. The floor was covered in blood as more and more people were killed. Every time I was in fear of it being me. Fifty people, the time for me to die was nearly here. Forty people, thirty, twenty, ten. When there were nine people left there were longer spaces between each death. Three people left. A longer space, I realised... it was my turn.

Samuel Best (8)
Cawood CE Primary School, Cawood

Kilmel, The Dark Wizard

In the shadows, a figure stood waiting for Peter to approach, but he turned away. The figure came out and it was the evil dark wizard, Kilmel. Kilmel had vowed he would one day kidnap Peter and turn him into his slave. Back at his castle, he made a spell to teleport him to Peter. A long, furious battle took place. Kilmel fired deadly spells towards Peter. Peter managed to dodge them all, finally Peter clawed his way to a sword, stabbing him in the heart. Peter became a hero. The city had an enormous feast and lived happily again.

Dylan Davenport (8)
Cawood CE Primary School, Cawood

Charlie The Dragon Slayer

I heard a deafening roar. "I'm going to check what it is! A dragon! He is red and very big with enormous wings, monstrous claws, the biggest, reddest eyes I've ever seen and the worst terrifying teeth! My name is Super Charlie. I am super strong and mega fast and ready to slay this monster. It's not going to be an easy task but I will be courageous and defeat this dragon once and for all." Slowly I crept up whilst he was in a deep slumber not knowing I was about to pounce on him. "Here we go..."

Charlie Holdcroft (8)

Cawood CE Primary School, Cawood

The Horse Adventure

As I galloped on my horse I had to find my lost parents with my friends Abby and Lola. By the way, I am called Lucy. After loads of stopping and starting, we found ourselves at a little village called Cawood. It had a little shop and school and a small cottage where we stayed. When we went in I noticed something at the till that looked familiar. I looked at my photo of my parents and looked back up. I stepped closer and closer, it was my parents. "Yay." I had found them finally. "I am so happy."

Alana Thorpe (10)
Cawood CE Primary School, Cawood

Santa's Delivery

One foggy Christmas Eve Santa was getting the reindeer ready and loading all of the presents onto the sleigh. He set off into the dark gloomy night. He had done Germany and Greece but then whilst he was flying to Spain he crashed into a cliff. Hanging on for dear life on an upside down sleigh. What was Santa going to do? But he had an idea. Shimming across the sleigh trying not to slip, he got onto Rudolph and set off to deliver all of the other presents to different people. Just him and Rudolph. They did it.

Alex Needham
Cawood CE Primary School, Cawood

The Disappointed Pirates

We sailed for months to the boiling tip of Africa. Being a pirate is the life for me, sailing all over the world. We have been following an ancient, ripped map for years, it's so old we can't really read it. When we got to where the X was marked we dug and dug in the soft sand until we hit something big and hard. But when we lifted the massive treasure chest and opened it, it was empty. Someone had got the treasure before me and my tired crew, we all thought it was a waste of our lives.

Daisy Lawrence (8)
Cawood CE Primary School, Cawood

The Day I Travelled

Falling quickly down the dark damp hole time fell still. I wondered where it was taking me. Seconds ago I was in my garden. Now I was lifting my head, looking up at Cawood Castle, I see it every day but today it looked different, it was newer and bigger. I knew where I was, but not when I was. In front of me there was a Viking warrior. Big, strong and straight from battle. He looked at me but couldn't see me. On the ground, I saw a hoard of treasures. I stashed it in my pockets and ran!

Elizabeth Dean
Cawood CE Primary School, Cawood

The Magic Island

The lights flickered, the room shook and a strange wind blew, it took us to a large deserted island with a small map (that was on the floor) with a mark to show us where the treasure was. On our way, we dodged thousands of falling coconuts, lots of swooping birds and big sharks and dolphins leaping over the island. There was a big treasure box, we all crowded round with great excitement. I carefully lifted the lid and we all gasped...

Megan Stephenson (9)
Cawood CE Primary School, Cawood

The Magic Mystery

As we were about to set off on the adventure the leader said, "Okay, is everyone ready? Remember it is a dangerous mountain we are taking you to so be careful." Everyone was bent down, their heads were facing north but their bodies were facing east. One hand was empty but the other had a large spear five feet big but as sharp as a machete. This adventure was about a gemstone in the mountain. We were scrambling up the humongous pearl-white mountain with frosty snow up ahead. We saw something shining. "Oh my gosh is that the gem?"

Effie Ellwood (10)
Danesfield CE School, Williton

The Dangerous Depths...

"Tanya? Tanya?" he called. There was no response. A wave of anxiety flushed over him. He tried speeding up through the bog, but there was too much mud. He couldn't survive on his own. "She can't be gone..." He swore she was right ahead a moment ago. He shoved the tough layer of plants out of his way. He took one step forward, onto a pile of leaves and he fell. It felt as if he was falling for hours, weeks... Then he landed with a splash. He stared around carefully. There she was! Her lifeless body, right there...

Ruby D'Alcorn (10)
Danesfield CE School, Williton

The Arctic Gem

In a frozen icy landscape, lived two friends, a polar bear and an Arctic fox.

For years and years, they have heard stories about the legend of the Arctic gem and its power to reverse climate change. One day the two friends wandered off into the icy land of the Arctic to find the Arctic gem. On the journey, they tackled many obstacles and it became clear the Arctic gem was not on land! They called upon their friend the narwhale who could use his large tusk to dig into the underwater icecaps. He found the gem shining with power.

Grace Mcloughlin (10)
Danesfield CE School, Williton

The Lost Dog

Once upon a time, very long ago, three days ago, there was a lost dog. The name of the dog was Archie. Archie was a very good dog until he went missing. His owner was really sad but the owner set off to find Archie. The owner couldn't find Archie so he gave up. Then he got a feeling that Archie was near so he went off again. He was sure that he could find Archie and he did. The owner saw Archie was in the park and the owner was really happy.

Evie James-Allen (9)
Danesfield CE School, Williton

The Adventure Of The Sheep

One day Freddy the sheep broke away from the flock in search of an adventure. He went into the woods and had an epic day scratching on trees and finding new stuff. When it got dark a fox started attacking Freddy. For a while, Freddy lay there unconscious.

The next day the shepherd was counting his sheep and he went into the forest and found him. He took him back to the farm to get him back to full health.

Thomas Ellicott (9)
Danesfield CE School, Williton

Leah And The Jaguar King

As the sun sets upon the horizon the jaguar rises as its prey is near. Leah sets off on an adventure. Dressed in tweed and leather boots she marched. Scouting her town, she found a passageway covered in cobwebs; Leah wasn't too sure about entering. She read the sticky note on the door. It said... 'Enter If You Dare'! She opened the door; as it creaked, there right in front of her eyes stood the animal himself, Scar, the jaguar king. She pulled out the pocket knife she'd gotten for her birthday and fought. Suddenly Scar fell to the ground.

Heidi Edmondson
Ennerdale CE Primary School, Ennerdale Bridge

Treasure Canyon

It's a sunny day at the Grand Canyon and Harry, Jack and I are enjoying the sun. Suddenly Jack stood up to find a treasure map under his feet. He told me and Harry about his great discovery. We excitedly gathered everything we needed and together we all started to trek alongside the extraordinary Grand Canyon.

After one exhausting hour of hiking the map said to cross a bridge, it was a wobbly rope bridge. We all precariously walked across the bridge, it was a real nightmare. Eventually, we found the treasure. As happy as anything we all went home!

George Lister (9)
Ennerdale CE Primary School, Ennerdale Bridge

The Treasure Map

One night I was tidying my room and I found a treasure map. "Lady," I called, "look at this!" It was a gloomy night outside, so I packed a bag of supplies and then set off to the Rocky Mountains with Lady (my adventure dog). Wasting no time, I ran to get her lead. "Come on, let's go." She bounded out of the door.

Surrounding the waterfall was the Rocky Mountains. We raced down the hill and there it was. A tsunami was due that day. "Oh no, Lady we've run into trouble, come on let's get out of here!"

Jessie Torrance (8)
Ennerdale CE Primary School, Ennerdale Bridge

The Girl With Long Hair

Forty years ago a young girl named Stephanie had 40,0000m of hair.

Now you might think this is cool but Stephanie causes an extraordinary amount of accidents but tripping over was the main accident. Another problem at school was that she was teased for having no family. This upset her so she left school. She went shopping and changed completely. Then she went to the jungle to see what terrors she could slay. She did it to show boys girls are better. Thanks to her girls and boys are now treated equally. It's all thanks to heroic Stephanie.

Olivia Hyland

Ennerdale CE Primary School, Ennerdale Bridge

Back To The Past

It was the night of Friday 22nd December 1992. In Fye Manor only one light could be seen, the light from Armituis' room. Exactly six months ago he had an encounter with fairies. Now when you think of fairies I bet you think of cute things with wings... That's wrong, they are mean and horrible with pointy ears and they carry weapons! Because they were so bad Armituis had to go back in time, back to 1100 when the first fairy was standing in front of him. Armituis killed the fairy with his sword and then came back and celebrated!

Annabelle Fye (10)
Ennerdale CE Primary School, Ennerdale Bridge

The Golden Pig

It was deafening in the cockpit. Dick had been travelling by helicopter for hours... Suddenly the helicopter started to splutter and fall. As they dropped Dick spotted... an island! They were going to hit it! After the collision, Dick found himself lying on a beach surrounded by Rouge Piglins (pig men). It was like they all started running after him, with spears! This meant a car chase but with no cars. As he ran he stumbled upon a golden pig!

So as you would, he slowly mounted on it and amazingly teleported home! I know weird right?

Elwood Park (10)
Ennerdale CE Primary School, Ennerdale Bridge

The World Championships

I was racing in Portimao, Portugal at The World Championships. Leading the race by a hair width as we came onto the beach sector... *Bang!* I crashed as a tsunami came onto the beach. A pig in a swimsuit came flying in, kicked me in the head... I went into an unknown world. It was almost as if it was the future. The island had lots of robots on it but they weren't robots, they were androids. I asked one, "How do I return to the race track?" I was World Champion and I was very happy with the result.

Jorge Edgar (11)
Ennerdale CE Primary School, Ennerdale Bridge

The Rainbow Key

There was a girl called Lily, she was in bed but when she woke up she was in a cave, she was scared. There were loose rocks ahead but she didn't realise they were loose. She walked deeper into the cave and stepped on one. She then realised they were loose and jumped over them. She got over them. She suddenly saw lava in the distance, she knew what to do, she was going to make a bridge across the lava. She knew she was looking for the rainbow key and found it. She headed back and finally got home.

Beatrice Parkinson (8)
Ennerdale CE Primary School, Ennerdale Bridge

Once Upon A Time In The Year Of 2012

Once upon a time in the year of 2012, there was a normal day until... I heard something in the distance so I looked outside my window and there was a huge wave destroying everything in its path. I instantly sprinted away. I had heard of a doomsday bunker nearby so I ran there... When I got there I saw a few other people there too. I jumped in with them and waited for it to hit. After that, something else happened. More disasters came like meteors, lava and a tornado but we were safe here for now.

Stanley Baxter (9)
Ennerdale CE Primary School, Ennerdale Bridge

The Fire Dragon

Once upon a time, on a volcano island, there was a fire dragon with molten hot fiery breath. Anyone who trespassed was, well, killed! So one day I bravely went to check it out. When I got on the island the only thing that stood out to me was the colossal volcano with steps all the way up it. I ran through the forest hurtling past lots of threats, eventually getting to the top steps. I saw no adult dragon but a baby. I tamed the little creature and took it home to my base of operations.

George Stitt (8)
Ennerdale CE Primary School, Ennerdale Bridge

Serpent Man

One day, seventy thousand years ago, there was a kid named Jude, who was a black belt in karate. He loved dinosaurs! So one day he went on a quest to find them. While he was walking he saw a chest. It was glowing! He opened the glowing chest and it turned him into Serpent Man! Just then he met some ninjas and then Serpent Man said, "Rise my serpents, rise!" Serpents then came blasting out of the ground and they defeated the ninjas in a second!

Jude Naven (8)
Ennerdale CE Primary School, Ennerdale Bridge

The Petrifying Forest

A girl called Emily was walking peacefully through the forest. Suddenly, a rustle behind her. Sharply turning around lurking behind her was a tiger. Behind the stripy tiger was the silhouette of a witch. It had stepped into the light. Emily was petrified. She ran faster than she had ever ran before. She ran until she came to a house. As Emily walked into the house the door shut behind her...

Nieve Fye
Ennerdale CE Primary School, Ennerdale Bridge

The Ice Monster

It all started when I wanted to uncover the truth about the ice monster. I had no choice. It was now or never. The big night had arrived. This was the time when I had to let my fearful fantasy take me to the frozen kingdom. Terrified but excited, I began my journey across the dangerous, snowy mountain. Suddenly, warning signs about the ice monster were appearing everywhere. But I didn't care. My palms were shivering, my head was aching, my heart was pounding. Courageously, I stood and stared. Had I discovered the truth or had the ice monster won?

Fabian Gontaru
Fairway Primary School, Mill Hill

My Journey To Find Treasure

I was sold a map. I realised it was a treasure map. I didn't know if it was real or not but decided to find out by going on the journey. I saw that the treasure was going to be hard to get. I got prepared with hiking equipment. I had to climb mountains. Later, I found two caves. One of them would lead to the treasure. I decided to check them both. First I went into the cave on the right. There was a chest in there. Nothing was in it. There was a rockfall. I was trapped forever.

Maryam Gitey
Fairway Primary School, Mill Hill

The Pokémon's Truth

One terrible day there was a boy named Josh who was not anywhere he knew... Suddenly there was an alien which dropped him out of a round-shaped UFO! Now it transformed into Eturnatis and Josh found a Charmander in a Pokéball in his pocket. Once Josh landed he saw Ash fighting Zacian. Suddenly Mewtwo came, looked at the UFO and said, "Nope, I'm out"
Then Goh showed up. He looked furious and said, "Come on." Josh looked confused. He realised he was in the World of Pokémon. Josh knew he had to get out but he couldn't...

Olly Pender (9)
Glenboig Primary School, Glenboig

The Truth

There once was a girl named Skyler, she was ten with blonde hair and blue eyes. Skyler had one sibling that she knew about and she enjoyed being the oldest because she could take her sister for walks. Skyler heard her mum on the phone to someone and it was on speaker. She peeked through the door and saw it said Skyler's brother. Skyler asked her mum, "Why were you on the phone with someone called Skyler's brother?" "It's a brother that I have never told you about. I'm sorry I didn't tell you about him," she replied.

Hollie Wood (9)
Glenboig Primary School, Glenboig

Cody's Adventure

A boy called Cody saw a glowing box with a note saying. 'Please help my kingdom, you have until sunset'. Cody set off to pack a bag for his journey. He went into the box. He seemed to be in the jungle. He had to move quickly, the sun was going down minute by minute. He came to a temple. He went inside, there was a chest with a note saying, 'You saved my kingdom'. He went into the chest and was finally home. "What a day," he said.
"There you are," Mum said.
"Hi," said Dad with a wink...

Tianna Hornal (9)
Glenboig Primary School, Glenboig

The Daring Rescue

Alola's BFF Athena was lost on a tall mountain.
She was counting on Alola to rescue her. Alola had
to travel many miles to get to where her friend
was. When she finally arrived, she realised how
high she had to go. But bravely, Alola didn't give
up. So up she climbed. Eventually, she reached the
top. She saw Athena, chomping a Milky Bar and
gazing out at the sky. She saw Alola and sprinted
towards her. She gave her a hug. Alola said, "We
better get down." They raced down. They both
waved goodbye and went back home.

Abigail Doig (9)
Glenboig Primary School, Glenboig

The Note

I climbed out of the sinking ship, cutlass raised, charging at the other ship. I leapt off of the wooden rail onto the other ship, plunging my cutlass into their floorboards. I reached out for the cannon and thrashed my cutlass against the fuse which immediately burst out into flames. A large iron ball suddenly blasted out of the end of the cannon, then exploded, sending wooden debris flying. A large blinding flash appeared as a cloud of dust and smoke rose in the air. Then a note drifted down to my feet like a feather falling in the sky.

Cameron Shaw (10)
Glenboig Primary School, Glenboig

Hunter Turtle

One day, Sam Turtle swam across the ocean to see her friend Molly. Molly was a hunter like Sam. They both lived in the shallow area of Blackpool beach. Their dream was to go to the deep end so one day Molly said, "Let's do it, let's go to the depths." Sam was scared at first but Molly was with her. They hopped on the boys' boat and headed off. As they jumped off, a shark swam up to Molly and stayed there till there was a sudden movement. "Don't turn around," said Sam. Suddenly Sam stabbed the shark.

Jane Mitchell (10)
Glenboig Primary School, Glenboig

The Arctic Mon

One frosty, freezing day a man named Monster Hunter was forty-one. He had rusty old leather armour and a shining shield and sword. He loved the Arctic, but the ship that he uses sunk. He was stranded in the Arctic, but he can handle the drafty island. While trembling through the cold snow he heard a *roar*. It was coming from a frosted, foggy cave. Monster Hunter went in and saw an Arctic mon, he pulled out his sword and started attacking. The beast had a frozen blast but Monster Hunter hit that blast away and won the fight!

Murdo Neil (9)
Glenboig Primary School, Glenboig

Slayer

Finally, I have captured the element of fire. I could feel it running through my body. I could finally beat my opponent. "I'm Mike the mighty slayer, I will beat the scorpion shooting venom from its big claws fast. It's a worthy opponent. I have an obsidian armour steel sword. Here is the castle I shall enter. Wow, this place is extraordinary, it's so spacious. Who's there? It must be the enemy." As I ran through the hallway it was feasting on something facing me. As it ran at me I sliced its neck easily.

John Brown (10)
Glenboig Primary School, Glenboig

Catching Bob The Baddie

I raced to the empty cell. I peeked in and the cell was open. It was dark with bats in the corner. I looked at the door and it said the name, Bob. I couldn't believe my eyes. I ran as quick as the Flash. I looked for Bob all over the place. Five hours later I still couldn't find Bob. Then I went to McDonald's for dinner. I looked over at the next table and it said reserved for Bob. Just as I went to order I caught him eating a quarter pounder with fries and a chocolate milkshake.

Emma Kennedy (10)
Glenboig Primary School, Glenboig

Slaying The King Gorilla

One sunny day there was a little boy called Kieran and he decided to explore a jungle. He finally found a jungle so he went in. The first thing he saw was a tree frog on a tree next to a pond. Then he saw a massive gorilla standing on a tree stump. Kieran ran as fast as he could. Then he saw the gorilla lunging towards him and Kieran grabbed a sharp stick and threw it at the gorilla. The gorilla got even madder so Kieran just decided to attack the gorilla and the gorilla died.

Kieran Cummings (9)
Glenboig Primary School, Glenboig

A Jungle Curse

As a cold breeze blew between the trees of the jungle, Misty entered the jungle. She looked around her surroundings and saw a stream, she followed the stream that took her to a jungle temple. She looked at the temple in shock. Her fur bristled, but she shook the fear away and told herself, "I'm not scared, I've been through everything." She went into the temple. When she entered it looked as if a hurricane had hit the place. She stepped on something...

Ala Mleczak (10)
Glenboig Primary School, Glenboig

A Magic Book

There once was a girl called Jemma. She was at school and she went to her locker and found a weird book that she did not put there. Her BFF Olivia brought the book to class. Jemma looked through the book and it was all blank so she wrote... 'I want a puppy and I want a new puppy for my BFF too' into it. Later on that day she went home from school and there was a puppy on the couch. Also, her BFF had a puppy on her bed too. The girls loved the puppies.

Jemma Pickering (9)
Glenboig Primary School, Glenboig

The Jungle Warrior

I entered the thick jungle. It was dark and swampy. There was rustling in the bushes. Suddenly a Burmese python slid out and tried to bite me. I ran for my life. Luckily I found a lodge so I hid in it for a while. I saw a sword, shield, bow and arrow. I picked them up and ran out the door, cut the python and climbed a tree. While the python was in pain I shot it with an arrow. It slithered into the river. I climbed down from the tree. Little did I know...

Connor Maloney (10)

Glenboig Primary School, Glenboig

The Jungle

In a dark old jungle, I was walking when I suddenly fell into a hole. I felt a splash on my back. I felt like I fell on something. I did, it was a curse. I transformed into a giant leopard. I felt petrified. Then I heard a sound in the bushes. It was a... little baby leopard. It was lost. I helped it. Then I heard a human and I ran to the safest place possible. I kept the young one safe. I heard my mum call. It was dinner time but I was still a leopard!

Rhona Struzik (10)
Glenboig Primary School, Glenboig

Jodie And Abigail's Adventure

In my bedroom I found a box with a necklace and my birth certificate. My sister came in and I told her what I had found. We went to find the truth. I put on the necklace and my hands went on fire. "Argh!" I said. Finally, it stopped. We found a cave. We found a clue. It said... 'To find the truth you need to find six clues, then the truth will be revealed'...

Jodie Taylor (10)
Glenboig Primary School, Glenboig

The Brave Treasure Hunter

Hi, I'm Adventurous Amelia. I was following the famous Serco's treasure map, which led to the cave of the jungle. I could almost smell the treasure so I thought I would find it with much ease. "Argh! A tiger!" I sprinted through the terrifying tiger's territory, my heart racing. Further, into the jungle's hidden cave, I was filled with joy to see a glorious pile of 15 diamonds, 200 gold coins and 100 sapphires! It was that moment when I wanted to faint in elation. Thankfully, I had a safe journey home and locked the treasure in my secret cabinet.

Pranav Khurana (8)
Handcross Park School, Handcross

The Useless Plane Trip

I took my seat next to an elderly lady. I knew that I was heading towards the thief's base. Unfortunately, the seats were as hard as rocks. Clare (the lady sitting next to me) brought up an interesting conversation when the loudspeakers announced this, "The engine is having a bit of trouble but please remain seated." Clare looked panicked and I was about to comfort her when she rushed to the emergency door and jumped! Luckily she had a parachute on but then something hit me in the face, a grey lady's wig! Oh that thief, he'd gotten away again.

Maggie Lunn (10)
Handcross Park School, Handcross

The Treasure Hunters

In an ordinary world that was not that ordinary, there was once a geologist who wished that he could go to an underwater city. He gathered a group and they were called The Treasure Hunters. They brought a sausage dog. They had adventures at the savanna, Nepal and Mars, but never below sea! The geologist was sad. One day, in the mail, the government allowed underwater travel. The group bought a million pound boat capable of above and below water travel. Finally, they found the underwater city and found treasure, but they got attacked by the people who lived there!

Zac Jones (8)
Handcross Park School, Handcross

The Treasure Box

I had a vision of treasured gems hidden beneath the thick vines growing by the old emergent tree. My dream ended when I found a wonderful treasure box and gasped in astonishment at my find.

The next day, I visited the emergent tree and I found the thick lime green vines. I took my rucksack off my back and pulled out a sharp knife. I slashed the vines away and underneath was a glittering jewelled box. The box was covered in emerald and sapphire gems. Suddenly, something hit my head. It was a walnut. There were monkeys everywhere, grinning cheekily.

Aneira Cook (8)
Handcross Park School, Handcross

Spooky Afternoon

One spooky afternoon we were in a deserted graveyard. It was so foggy. We were exploring for treasure, but instead, we saw 6,000 ghosts! It was scary for me, but not for them.

They said, "Helloooooo!" They actually helped us, leading us through the graves to the old tree where we found treasure! It was very exciting. We tugged it up and opened the box of treasure: it was a big surprise! There were beautiful dresses and lots of sparkly jewels. We quickly dressed up and put the jewellery on, in time for the ball. We danced and had fun!

Tennessee Milkins
Handcross Park School, Handcross

Behind A Waterfall

Behind a waterfall grew a magic flower which revealed an everlasting power. Two girls, Esa and Ruth, were on a journey to find it. The two swooped and slid across rocks and reeds until they reached the waterfall. The water glimmered in delight as they stared in amazement. They started weaving the water in a golden brown boat, palm leaves and flowers decorated its edges. They glided up the waterfall. As they reached the top, a petal of the flower floated into their hands. They felt the magic swirl around them and drifted home on magic golden leaves.

Shreya Chitrapu (8)
Handcross Park School, Handcross

Mission Ghost

I was in a graveyard (by the way I am a superhero on a mission) trying to find the ghost who needed help. I had heard the ghost. I was quite near to it when it started to make an ear-piercing sound.
I went over and said, "Hi, I am here to help! What do you need help with?"
The ghost suddenly said, "Helllllooooooo! My name is Gurtruuuude and I need help with getting a friend."
"Okay, I can help with that," I said.
"Oooooh thanks, but how will I get one?"
"Well, I can be your friend!" I replied.

Lucy Flatt
Handcross Park School, Handcross

The Flying Map

A girl and a boy went walking. They found a map and decided to follow it. The boy put the map in his pocket, but, when he looked again, it wasn't there! They had lost the map and they had no way home! The girl spotted a building: it looked abandoned and they walked closer. They went in and heard mysterious voices. There were two people. The boy gulped and said, "Excuse me? Do you know the way to Rainbow Rusper? We are lost."
The men replied, "There is no such place as Rainbow Rusper!" How would they get home?

Harriet Higginson (8)
Handcross Park School, Handcross

Perfect Pirates

One morning, a young pirate named Pippa woke up to a beautiful sunrise. Her little boat drifted across an ocean blue lake that shone brightly in the sun. She sleepily walked across to her little kitchen and then, as she got the egg out of the fridge, she saw a letter. Pippa carefully opened it. Inside it told Pippa to search the mysterious lake. So without eating, she went into the lake and searched. She looked and then she found a rare flower that she needed. She was really happy! She had done it. Pippa ran inside with the flower!

Evie Gilbey (9)
Handcross Park School, Handcross

Ahana And The Curse

Once upon a time, there was a girl called Ahana. She was adventurous. One day a curse fell on Ahana's village and it got to Ahana's mum! Ahana's mum was the only one she had after her dad passed away and her mum was going to suffer the same fate, but just as Ahana was about to say goodbye, she remembered the village's healing flower. Ahana bolted to the emperor and asked if she could have the flower. He said, "Yes, but only if you give me that rare crystal in your house," and she did it for her mother.

Aroha Jagnale (8)
Handcross Park School, Handcross

A Gold Bird

The phoenix is a legendary bird born from fire. It has rainbow feathers and a beautiful voice. I never thought I would see a phoenix in real life, until one day a phoenix suddenly appeared! I was in an old forest when it said to me, "Find me and find great treasure beyond your wildest dreams!" Then the phoenix disappeared and I ran and ran! Suddenly, a rainbow feather floated down and I touched it expecting gold but instead, it was an adorable baby phoenix. It had no claws and a chirp like gold. It was a lovely baby!

Leo Howells (8)
Handcross Park School, Handcross

The Sacred Star Of Riannah

Gemma awoke in the helicopter. She got up and limped towards the pyramid. The Sacred Star hung at her neck. She edged along the edge of the pyramid and her hand slowly found a hole. She dived through, being careful of her leg. Inside was a massive hall, with coffins lined up. On a stand, was the cushion of the Sacred Star. As she limped towards it, she heard shouts and started to run. She placed the Star on the cushion and breathed a sigh of relief. Her mission was complete. She was free of her curse of the mummies.

Florence Clusker-Artemis (9)

Handcross Park School, Handcross

The Magic Flower

Once upon a time, in an underwater city called Magical City, there lived a mermaid called Coral. Coral was an adventurer and she was looking for a rare flower. She was on an important mission to find it.

One day she packed her things and set out to find the flower in the sea. When she finally found the flower she stopped to eat because it was lunch. Suddenly, she felt a wave of magic going through her and then she set off back home.

A few days later she was attacked by a shark and was never seen again.

Cecilia Rivera (9)
Handcross Park School, Handcross

Underground

Someone called Tiler was going underground with the Ragnarok. A Ragnarok is a humongous beast, whose head is as big as a classroom, in a massive cave. I heard some loud footsteps around me and I was scared. I heard a loud roar and some rubble fell from the ceiling. I ran up the cobwebbed stairs to see what was making the noise. To my amazement, I saw an injured Ragnarok lying on the floor kicking his legs. I asked what the matter was. I had learnt his language. He said, "I've badly hurt my hand."

Angus Weightman (8)
Handcross Park School, Handcross

Just A Dream?

I was lying in bed when suddenly there was a buzzing noise from under my bed. I was scared but interested. I carefully climbed out of bed and looked underneath. To my astonishment, there was a portal! I wanted to jump into it. A million questions flew through my head. *Should I jump, or not?* After a few minutes, I decided to jump. I landed on an island. There was a cave and some treasure! I saw another portal and It took me to the Queen! As soon as I delivered it I woke up: it was all a dream.

Henry Sheikh (8)
Handcross Park School, Handcross

Italy's Secret Temple

Once there was an ancient temple in Italy. A girl called Amy decided to explore it. It had palm trees and beautiful flowers. She had heard things about the temple. Gold was hidden right in the centre. She had a walk. Then she came to a river. The gold was on the other side but there were crocodiles in the river. Amy looked around for something to help. Amy saw a plank of wood and set it up. She walked across it trying not to wobble. When she got to the chest of gold, she opened it. It was beautiful.

Chloe Dawson (8)
Handcross Park School, Handcross

The Lost Temple

Dressed in black from head to toe the thief crept into the temple. He had dodged the swinging spiky ball and run through the passage. He clutched his bottle of poison, looked around and smirked. He had been very clever to get this far. All of a sudden the room began to flood with water. The emperor had spotted him! He held his breath but found he had no need to the water had all gone. Quickly he jumped up and ran through many more passages. He arrived, stepped in, but fell through the trap door.

Connie Lunn (9)
Handcross Park School, Handcross

The Black Panther

I arrived at a jungle house that was falling apart and I was scared. I came here on a mission for the Queen. I was trying to find some hidden treasure for her. She told me it was in this derelict house. It was horrible! Suddenly, I heard a creak and I saw a pair of bright yellow eyes and then out of the gloom I saw a black, hairy body and it turned into a hungry, angry panther. "Argh! Oh no!" I screamed. I ran as fast as I could away from the fierce, mighty panther. Would it follow?

Chloe Smith (8)
Handcross Park School, Handcross

The Creaky Door

I was in my bed on Halloween night when suddenly the door to my bedroom creaked open. A mysterious waft of air brushed across my face. I was curious and went onto the landing. Suddenly, a voice said, "Why are you here? This is my turf." "No, it is not! It is my house. Who are you and what are you doing here?" I tiptoed further onto the landing. Soon, I saw a monster! I was so scared that I hid in my bed for the whole of the night. It was a very, very scary night.

Lucy Clark (8)
Handcross Park School, Handcross

The Great Bank Robbery

One day after breakfast I decided to take a walk. I passed the bank and saw it was open, but I was puzzled as the bank isn't open on Sundays! Someone was in there! I crept inside and saw a robber! He was taking huge handfuls of money! He had thousands, thousands and thousands of pounds! I had to stop him immediately! I called the police on the number 999 emergency service! The police came immediately and dashed in like a blink of an eye! I looked back in but there was no one there!

Evelina Jansen
Handcross Park School, Handcross

A Mission For The Queen

I was on a battlefield when I got a mission from the Queen: it was to return some gems that had been stolen from Her Majesty. I started searching. Suddenly, I saw a suspicious guy with some gems in his pocket, so I ran, ran and ran. He ran into an old army shelter and I followed him inside. I saw three people so I ran into the shelter. One person ran out, but I grabbed the gems and put the thieves in jail. I brought the gems to the Queen and I got a shiny medal. It was amazing!

Harry Haswell (9)

Handcross Park School, Handcross

Portal To A World

One morning, when the sun was rising, I had a magnificent dream. It was a lovely day but then suddenly there was a portal! I stepped through the portal and I was on a lava stage! I felt like I was in a video game! I was so scared! I saw another portal ahead. I had to get there. When I reached it, there was this robot! I had to fight him so I grabbed a sword and smashed it. Suddenly, I teleported home. Someone called me up ahead and there was a monster. "Argh!"

Matilda Hewitt (8)
Handcross Park School, Handcross

Adventure Hunters

Flash! The TV went on.
"A plane crash happened in the jungle,"
announced the news.
"What? Wow!" shouted everyone. "That is cool."
"Let's go there!" said Jack.
"No, no!" said everyone.
"Come on, the police haven't gone yet, or
detectives!"
"Okay," said everyone with a moan.
"Yay!" said Jack.
Two minutes later...
"This is taking forever," said everyone sluggishly.
"Wait, look at that! It is right there!" shouted
everyone.
"Let's touch it," said Jack.
"Okay," said Tom, excited.
The touch was as hot as a volcano, but they saw a
waterfall, and then a monster popped out...

George Page (8)
Kennoway Primary School, Kennoway

Adventure Hunters

I woke up. I decided to on an adventure. I hope it's not scary. Firstly I need to get Jake.
Knock, knock!
"Jake, want to go on an adventure?"
"Yes, I do. Where? The park?"
"No, not there."
"Where do you want to go?"
"The abandoned hospital."
"Okay, let's go get a taxi to the city. Does your mum know?"
"Yes, she does."
"This place is tall."
"Of course it is. Are you ready to go in?"
"Yes, locked and loaded."
"Good. Anything could be in there. Dead people."
"Yes, there could."
"And zombies."
"Yes, that's why we're going..."

Cole Vanbeck (7)
Kennoway Primary School, Kennoway

Adventure Hunters

One day a brother and sister were walking in a forest. Joe said, "Oh no! We are lost!"
Ava said, "I see a cave in the distance."
"Let's go then!" exclaimed Joe.
Then they saw a huge shadow. They took a long stick and started to defend the cave... then they saw a glowing bottle. They picked it up.
Joe saw a mandrill and it was coming closer and closer.
Ava shouted, "Run!"
The cave was collapsing! Luckily they made it out just in time. "Phew!" said Ava. "Close one...
"Yeah," said Joe. "Let's get some berries to eat..."

Lyla Stevens (8)
Kennoway Primary School, Kennoway

Adventure Hunters

Once upon a time, a little girl found a key. Danni said, "I found a key! Cole, Kurtis, Angus, Jaimie, Ava, Emily and Kalyn come to the playground!" The key took them to a strange playground. A dinosaur appeared and everyone screamed and tried to get away.

"Why would we run? We should hide in that cave over there," said Danni.

"Help!" shouted Ava.

Ava tried to pull Angus and got him up but then fell. "Not again!" said Danni.

"It's not my fault, it is your fault Danni!" Ava shouted.

"Yes," said Emily.

They escaped to the cave.

Danni McFarlane (8)
Kennoway Primary School, Kennoway

The Tricks And Skills Circus

One day lots of people went to a circus. The circus was called the 'Tricks and Skills Circus'. The clown said, "Come in!" So everyone went in. Then the clown transported the people to an outside parkour place where you jump from building to building. Everybody wanted to do it. Everyone made the first building and all the other buildings. Then the clown took the people to the tallest mountain in the world! The clown said, "Is everybody ready for something insane?"
The people shouted, "Yes!" The clown did a backflip off the mountain. Everyone tried and had fun.

Nathan Scobie (8)
Kennoway Primary School, Kennoway

The Jungle Adventure

In the jungle, on a hot sunny day, Kieran and his two friends woke up in their cabin, in the perfect place. However, George was too hot so he went outside to get a breath of fresh air. Meanwhile, Georgina and Kieran watched television. Twenty-five minutes later, they decided to go check on him... He was nowhere to be seen! Suddenly, a giant wild lynx galloped out of the bush with George on his back! "Woohoo!" shouted George. "I'm back!" Kieran and his friends called the lynx, Laddie the lynx. They remained good friends for the rest of their lives.

Kieran Cramb (8)

Kennoway Primary School, Kennoway

Brilliant Bullion

One day two explorers were swimming in the ocean. Around them were bright pink and dark blue, colourful coral. When they were searching they came across an abandoned shipwreck. Slowly they swam inside and found the biggest, shiniest box of gold... shiny, sparkly gold bullion! Quickly they grabbed the bullion and swam to the surface. They hid the treasure inside a secret door on a huge palm tree. They decided to go back and search for precious gems. Sadly their tanks fell off their backs and they drowned.

Years later a lumberjack found the treasure... Lucky him!

Anna McMenigall (8)
Kennoway Primary School, Kennoway

Hunting Darnage

I was in the forest when I heard a weird noise. I was hunting Darnage with the army. *Crash!* A tree fell down. There was Darnage. He was covered in slimy acid.

An hour later, night fell and Darnage was climbing a tree. The whole forest was on fire and turning red. Flames rippled through the trees. Tanks started to arrive from the city, they were preparing to fire their cannons. Darnage stuck his long tongue out and the enormous tanks fired... The only dark sky was now filled with bright orange fireballs. Darnage caught fire and started to run...

Jake Smith (8)
Kennoway Primary School, Kennoway

Ramio's Treasure Hunt

Ramio woke up and on top of him was a map to discover special shiny treasure. The treasure was located at the bottom of the dark ocean. Ramio set off to find the enormous ocean. *Splash!* He jumped in and began to descend. Suddenly, the waves got bigger and bigger. In front of his eyes was a huge, fierce shark guarding the treasure. Ramio zapped the shark using his magical powers. The treasure was now his. Ramio opened the treasure. He couldn't believe his eyes. The chest was filled with diamonds and netherite, which lit up the dark ocean floor...

Corey Lambert (8)
Kennoway Primary School, Kennoway

Underwater Haunted House

Once there was a girl named Sofie. She was petrified when she heard the news about the haunted house...Then she phoned her friends about the haunted house. Her friends told her it was underwater. "Underwater?" she screamed. "It can't be!" They all gathered together, put their scuba stuff on and went scuba diving. When they reached the haunted house they went inside and found mysterious dust but they were underwater so how is there dust? They also found fangs... After they went to the lab and investigated. They were vampire fangs!

Lily McDougall (8)
Kennoway Primary School, Kennoway

Adventure Hunters

Tarzan was a fearless warrior. He was climbing up an erupting volcano, as he was being chased by Godzilla. This was because someone stole his massive box of cornflakes. Tarzan was furious, he had been starving! For miles, they ran but then Tarzan got stuck in sticky mud. Suddenly, the volcano exploded, it was blazing hot like the sun! Baby Zoda appeared and froze him and the lava. Luckily, Baby Zoda had an axe and made the cool lava crumble, meaning Tarzan was free! All this was for nothing because Tarzan dropped the cornflakes into the red-hot volcano!

Reilly Clader (8)
Kennoway Primary School, Kennoway

The Alien Adventure

Once upon a time, there were aliens in the City of Jelly. The city had the best galaxy jelly. This type of jelly gave the residents superpowers. Mr Jelly was in charge of the city and his superpower was one for all. This meant he could guard the city against intruders and stop them from entering. The aliens were trying to steal the city's galaxy jelly. Mr Jelly used his powers to protect the galaxy jelly from the aliens. The aliens could not win against Mr Jelly's superpowers so they retreated back to their home planet called The Stealers.

Gordon MacDonald (8)
Kennoway Primary School, Kennoway

Dangerous Adventures

In an enchanted forest Baby Yoda was holding his ears, he hated bagpipe noises! He saw the player, a scabby old man, wearing a Scotland top and a kilt. In his mind he thought, *oh no, this is dangerous! Crash!* went the bagpipes as Baby Yoda used his force to break the bagpipes. He never wanted to hear them again!

A few years later, he saw the Tartan Army and thought, *oh no, not again!* He turned around, hopped into his Ferrari and sped out of town, hot chilling all the way to China. "Phew, the bagpipes are done!"

Dean Galloway (8)
Kennoway Primary School, Kennoway

Mr Tickle And The Disappearing House

Mr Tickle was having a very good day. Twenty-one people were well and truly tickled, but when he arrived home, he couldn't believe his eyes. Someone had burnt down his house. Mr Tickle was really upset but also angry. He thought, *how could someone do this to me?* His house was gone. All there was, was a smoking charred pile. Mr Tickle dropped to his knees and tears started to roll down his cheeks. But then... along came Mr Happy to save the day. Behind him was an army of Mr Men. They had come to save Mr Tickle's day!

Kyan Ward (8)
Kennoway Primary School, Kennoway

Adventure Hunters

Bob and Billy were hunting for boars. They ran away. The boars were too strong so they ran to the house for some food. They were running out.

The next day they were starving! So they went hunting again with a magic staff and killed five boars. They were marvellously happy that they had food. They shouted, "Woohoo!"

They cooked the meat and ate the meat.

The next day they had a plan to kill a mammoth and they managed it. They used the staff but it did nothing.

After ten minutes they finally did it.

Oliver Love (8)

Kennoway Primary School, Kennoway

The Superhero Vs The Terrifying Tiger

The superhero was walking through the jungle. There were lots of tall trees and green leaves. He was looking all around and saw a terrifying tiger. *Roar!* The terrifying tiger jumped on the superhero from behind. The tiger tried to eat the superhero for his dinner but he used his powers and turned invisible. He ran as fast as an Olympic athlete to get out of the jungle. The tiger looked all around but the superhero was nowhere to be seen! He had disappeared from the jungle and was never caught by the terrifying tiger!

Bailey Bendex (8)
Kennoway Primary School, Kennoway

Adventure Hunters

I couldn't believe my eyes, because there was a big monster! And there was a big tarantula and a big shark in the water.
In the haunted hospital, an enormous bear ran at my back. I ran to get away from it.
I ran into the secret cave. There were millions of doors so I went in the first
door. Behind the first door, there was a big cave and there was an insanely big monster! "Oh help!" I shouted. I shouted at my friends. My friends ran to help me escape from the monster but one friend got caught...

Cole Innes (8)
Kennoway Primary School, Kennoway

An Abandoned School

One day, a long time ago, there was a school called Adventure Academy. All the greatest adventures happened there but it closed in the1970s. A girl called Alex was trying to Google it and she found a picture of an abandoned school. The next morning she and her friend Abbi decided to go and find the school. They finally arrived... The doors of the school shut but they didn't shut them! Then they started to look around and they went into the basement. They saw a portal and it led them to somewhere in the desert...

Madison MacKenzie (8)
Kennoway Primary School, Kennoway

Rob And The Koala

There once was a student called Rob. He was running through a vast and dark jungle. The wind was whistling through the tall trees. All of a sudden, at the top of a tree he heard loud snoring. Rob looked up and saw a cute, cuddly koala who was sound asleep. The strong wind suddenly blew the koala off of the branch. The koala started to fall and Rob rushed to catch him in his arms. Rob had saved the koala's life. Together they left the jungle and went to Rob's laboratory. The koala became his sidekick in the lab...

Molly Foster (8)

Kennoway Primary School, Kennoway

Mars Adventure

Wuggy Huggy made a toy rocket and filled it with fire. He blasted off! Bright orange flames filled the sky. He went into space and visited Mars. On Mars he found a robot called Carl, they stayed and played for five days. All around he could see stars and other planets. The planets were all different to look at but the sun was the brightest of them all. It was shining and was as hot as a flaming fire. Wuggy Huggy and Carl were getting closer to the sun on their adventure. They were getting hotter and started to burn...

Alexander Brook (8)

Kennoway Primary School, Kennoway

North Pole Adventure

The North Pole was covered in white snow and was really cold. As I walked through the thick snow, my footprints left a trail. I couldn't believe it, Santa, his main elf, Elfie and Rudolph were in the distance. I started to run towards them and Rudolph started to gallop towards me. I jumped on Rudolph's back and he took me to Santa and Elfie. Elfie pushed me off of Rudolph's back and I nearly fell face-first into the snow. But suddenly I was surrounded by golden dust! Santa had used his powers to save me.

Cameron Allen (8)
Kennoway Primary School, Kennoway

The Undiscovered Animal

One day Corey, Jake, Sean, Cameron and I discovered a vast forest. We decided to explore for undiscovered animals. We sneaked in and saw something move in the vast green tree. I felt excited but a wee bit nervous because I didn't expect to find something so soon. We were thinking about this when suddenly a branch fell off the tree. *Bang! Crash!* When I opened my eyes I saw a massive gorilla with four eyes and fifteen hungry mouths... It was terrifying! We ran for our lives and no one ever saw it again!

Finlay Brian Thomas Whyte (8)

Kennoway Primary School, Kennoway

Saving The Dolphin

One winter's night there was a monumental storm, all of the plastic was in the sea. Ten minutes later, the storm stopped. I went splashing into the sea to save the dolphin from the shark. The shark was angry because of the plastic that went in last night. The dolphin was deep below the surface so it was hard to save it but eventually I managed. It was a tiny dolphin but the shark was huge. I could hardly believe my eyes. The shark chomped but he couldn't catch me. I finally escaped out of the ocean alive.

Logan Mitchell (8)
Kennoway Primary School, Kennoway

Joe And The Scary Cave

Once upon a time, Joe was in the vast, dark woods. He closed his eyes and suddenly all he could hear was the whistling wind and tree branches falling. A storm was coming and Joe was terrified. He started to run away from the wind and discovered a huge cave. Joe ran inside but the cave was pitch-black. He couldn't see a thing. *Bang! Crash! Boom!* The rocks at the entrance of the cave tumbled down. There was no way out for Joe. He was trapped. The cold icy air started to fill the cave. Joe was alone...

Daria Dihoru (8)
Kennoway Primary School, Kennoway

Lava Is Dangerous

I discovered a volcano that suddenly erupted, throwing red-hot lava everywhere. Sadly, someone was hit by the lava and burnt their foot. I rushed to help her but it was too late, she was screaming in agony. "Argh!" I carefully lifted her up and carried her safely to the hospital. It was twenty-five miles away so my arms were sore like a bullet wound. They repaired her burnt foot and she was able to walk again. She visited me to say thank you and gave me a gigantic gorilla, that had to live in the zoo.

Harvey Barker (8)
Kennoway Primary School, Kennoway

The Clown

There once was a carnival downtown, two kids Rachel and Artie went to visit. When they got there they saw a clown was hiding something so they wanted to investigate. They saw the clown in the changing room and suddenly they were transported to Circus Land. It was atrocious and scary and last but not least it was smelly. Then they saw the clown. "Argh, run!"
"I am your enemy!" said the clown.
They ran behind the circus set-up and the clown didn't know where they had gone...

Kaitlyn Wilson (9)
Kennoway Primary School, Kennoway

The Arctic Age

In the Arctic the ice was melting and all of a sudden the ice went snap! The ice was as cold as a snowstorm. The adorable polar bears were terrified. I started running as I knew where we would be safe. *Thud! Thud!* The polar bears were chasing me. We arrived at the ocean's edge where there was a line of enormous boats. The polar bears and I rushed onto one of the boats and started sailing away from the melted ice. All of a sudden, I could see the giant waves approaching. A shark was coming...

Carly Lench (8)
Kennoway Primary School, Kennoway

Adventure Hunters

One day I was in my room and I heard a noise. *Bang!* I went to check. My mum was at her work so I phoned my mum and she picked me up. My little sister was crying because of the noise. Mum came home and tried to find out what made the bang. She decided to phone the police to come and see if anyone had broken in. A window had been smashed and someone had broken in and gone downstairs. Mum's silver bracelet had gone missing from the drawer.

The policeman went to try to find the burglar.

Lily Curran (7)
Kennoway Primary School, Kennoway

The Fierce Fox

I was walking to school when I heard a crack in the bushes. I went to check it out. As I got closer I discovered an orange fox. It pounced at me and I shouted, "Argh!" I started to sprint away but I didn't know where I was. The fox was getting closer. I saw Mrs Kilbane, who I asked for help. We went back into the forest together. The leaves under our feet were rustling and the wind was whistling. Now I had company I was no longer afraid of the fierce fox. I was ready to face him...

Frankie Barrie (8)
Kennoway Primary School, Kennoway

The Jungle

One morning I woke up in the jungle and I wondered where I was so I stood up and went for a walk. On my walk, I heard a noise behind me so I looked and I saw a lion... I ran as fast as I could until *bang!* I face-planted to the ground screaming, "I just want to be friends."
The lion said, "Okay."
After that, we played our favourite game, tig and we played it for hours. Then the tiger got angry and started to chase me but I escaped and never saw him again.

Amelie McAllister (8)
Kennoway Primary School, Kennoway

The Cave Monster

On Saturday it was a very stormy evening. I was in my bed when suddenly I heard a giant roar! It was coming from the cave next to my house. So, I went and got clothes and my hat, scarf and gloves. I got to the cave and the noise was getting closer and closer. Its eyes were flashing red! Then I heard a loud scream, something had caught someone! The monster came out of the cave. It was huge, there were bats and zombies! I started to run... I ran as fast as a cheetah but it wasn't enough...

Alana Nicholson (8)
Kennoway Primary School, Kennoway

Carmela And The Unicorn

Once upon a time, there was a princess called Carmela. She lived in a castle with her parents! She was always bored in the castle. She had a big house, she even had a unicorn. She was rich. The money was as gold as the sun. There was something in space. A meteor was going to hit the land but Carmela had an idea. Her idea was to try to save the land. She rode her unicorn to where the meteor would land, soon she could see it getting bigger and closer... the unicorn used magic to stop it!

Reese Dryden (8)
Kennoway Primary School, Kennoway

Lost In The Jungle

One day I was walking in the enormous jungle. All around me were giant trees and green leaves. The leaves were blowing everywhere like a tornado. It was a dark and stormy night, I was terrified. The rain started to pour so I tried to find my way back home. I looked to the left and to the right but I was lost! Every direction I looked had the same giant trees. I didn't know which way to go. I started to run as fast as a cheetah but I felt like I was running in circles. I was lost...

Sofie Anderson (8)
Kennoway Primary School, Kennoway

The Truth Of The Forest

The truth of the forest was a mystery for a long time...There is a hunter's cabin and Hunter Steve has a quest is find the truth of the forest but he's trying to find a pyramid that looks like a green tree. The hunter's cabin is camouflaged and he goes into the forest. He keeps looking and looking until he finds it. He is so happy. He goes in, it is very old with big spiderwebs. It is disgusting. He finds a gem that is blue and glowing. It looks dangerous so he walks away.

Oban Cation (8)

Kennoway Primary School, Kennoway

The Hospital Patient

Tick-tock, tick-tock... The hospital patient was transported to the House of Snow! All you could see was snow and ice. It was quite chilly for the patient. He was frozen and then he heard a voice saying, "What? Pardon? What did you say?" He felt like he was losing his mind a little and then he met someone called Dani. "You heard me," said Dani. "No I did not!" shouted the patient. All he could see was black and white... Was he a penguin?

Dani Curran (8)
Kennoway Primary School, Kennoway

The Colourful Fireworks

It was really dark and I set off to my mum's work. I could hear the bang of fireworks in the distance. The fireworks were lighting up the sky. The once dark sky became filled with rainbow colours. When I arrived, I found a huge blue glow stick. I put it around my neck and went to the beach. The beach was really sandy and I could hear the waves splashing. *Bang! Bang!* The sky filled with amazing colours. I couldn't believe my eyes... The fireworks were amazing!

Lewis Pile (8)
Kennoway Primary School, Kennoway

The World Of Candy Land

One day there was a boy named Bob and he loved candy. He dreamed of being in a place called Candy Land. When he was dreaming about it... a miracle happened. He teleported into Candy Land and he was as happy as a cat. He ran to a chocolate bar and took a big bite. his mouth was full of joy but he realised that the chocolate was supposed to be a bridge and it all fell. A gummy bear monster came and chased Bob around and Bob fell. *Crash!* The monster ate him all up...

Jayden Mackie (8)
Kennoway Primary School, Kennoway

The Forest

In the forest, there was a boy called Jack. He always went to the river. Jack lived in a castle. His parents were a queen and king. Jack and his parents were getting swept down the river to the beach. He played in the sand and his parents sunbathed in the sun. Then Jack went in the water and he surfed on the water, it was fun. He said for his parents to join him in the water. They loved it so much but then they went back to the forest and went on to a park.

Kaylin Robertson (8)
Kennoway Primary School, Kennoway

Adventure Hunters

We went to a forest and found a chest. In the chest, there was a note and a key. The note led us to a magic door. The key unlocked it and a storm came by. Charley, Amie, Lola and I ran inside as fast as we could.

There was another chest and inside was another note. The note led us to the forest again so we walked a different way and found a deer at the end of the forest. Something had happened to the deer's leg. It was bleeding so I took her home.

Cindi Bowman (8)
Kennoway Primary School, Kennoway

Adventure Hunters

Boom! A plane crashed. I ran into a cabin and got my tools. I fixed the plane and drove it to an abandoned police station. I found an old bat. It was about to be a zombie apocalypse so the bat will come in handy.

Vroom! A car shot past. I needed to get my hands on the car for the apocalypse so I followed the car and the man dropped the keys. I grabbed them and ran to the vehicle. I got in it and I drove it. The zombies appeared...

Derri Seath (8)
Kennoway Primary School, Kennoway

The Magic Stick

One day my mum, dad and I went to a beach. It had a scary forest behind it. I went in, I was so scared. A few minutes later I tripped. When I tripped I found a stick, it was glowing so I went back to the beach. When I was at the beach I started floating in the air but I said to myself, "Go down," and I went down. I thought it must have been a magic stick. I then went home and discovered more magical powers. What could I use these for next?

Darcey Richards (8)
Kennoway Primary School, Kennoway

Sun And Snow

There was once a town and it was always sunny. The Sun Queen lived there. She loved the sun until a Frost Queen came and took over everything. She took my best friend Joe, this is how I got him back... I went to find a really warm jacket and I went to save the sun. I went into a cave. I could hear, "Help me!" I thought it could be Joe and I was furious! Plot twist... I'm the Sun Queen...

Annalise Allan (9)
Kennoway Primary School, Kennoway

The Monster Machine

The monster machine began to shake. *Bang!* The monster came out as Dinosaur Boy. He had sharp spikes on his back and his eyes were as green as the bogey monster. He had a big tail, long like a snake. He went to destroy the school with his big long tail. He swung it about. *Crash!*

Blake Curran (8)

Kennoway Primary School, Kennoway

YOUNG WRITERS INFORMATION

We hope you have enjoyed reading this book – and that you will continue to in the coming years.

If you're a young writer who enjoys reading and creative writing, or the parent of an enthusiastic poet or story writer, do visit our website **www.youngwriters.co.uk**. Here you will find free competitions, workshops and games, as well as recommended reads, a poetry glossary and our blog. There's lots to keep budding writers motivated to write!

If you would like to order further copies of this book, or any of our other titles, then please give us a call or order via your online account.

Young Writers
Remus House
Coltsfoot Drive
Peterborough
PE2 9BF
(01733) 890066
info@youngwriters.co.uk

Join in the conversation!
Tips, news, giveaways and much more!

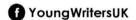 **YoungWritersUK**    **YoungWritersCW**   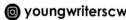 **youngwriterscw**